2/02

Palo Alto City Library

The individual borrower is responsible for all library material borrowed on his or her card.

Charges as determined by the CITY OF PALO ALTO will be assessed for each overdue item.

Damaged or non-returned property will be billed to the individual borrower by the CITY OF PALO ALTO.

P.O. Box 10250, Palo Alto, CA 94303

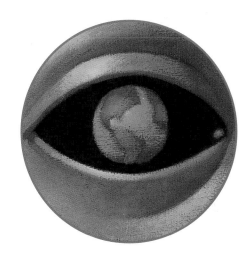

Out of the Everywhere

TALES FOR A NEW WORLD

○

JAN ANDREWS

ILLUSTRATED BY

Simon Ng

A GROUNDWOOD BOOK

DOUGLAS & McINTYRE

TORONTO VANCOUVER BUFFALO

Groundwood Books / Douglas & McIntyre
720 Bathurst Street, Suite 500
Toronto, Ontario M5S 2R4

Distributed in the USA by Publishers Group West
1700 Fourth Street
Berkeley, CA 94710

We acknowledge the financial support of the Canada Council for the Arts, the Ontario Arts Council and the Government of Canada through the Book Publishing Industry Development Program for our publishing activities.

Canadian Cataloguing in Publication Data
Andrews, Jan
Out of the everywhere : tales for a new world
"A Groundwood book".
ISBN 0-88899-402-8
I. Ng, Simon. II. Title.
PS8551.N37097 2000   jC813'.54   C00-931265-X
PZ7.A52Ou 2000

Design by Michael Solomon
Printed and bound in China by Everbest Printing Co. Ltd.

CONTENTS

To the young listener who kept saying, "Tell us more stories from here."

FOREWORD

Long ago, storytellers were often also wanderers, carrying tales from place to place. In those days, the stories were written in people's hearts and minds instead of on pages. This meant that the ways of the words were less fixed. Themes and patterns might be kept steady, but much else was open to change.

Following in the footsteps of those long-ago tellers, I have taken tales that have come to us through the heritage of our various cultural communities. I have reset those tales in our own landscape, hoping they will become part of our own folk culture in their time.

The title of the book is part of the answer to a question I used to ask my mother when I was little. "Where did I come from?" I would say to her, and she would always answer, "Out of the everywhere into here." My dream is that "into here" is where these tales are going, but I know I cannot accomplish the dream alone.

These are tales for the telling. In fact, they need to be retold and reshaped over and over if they are to come fully to life. So, breathe them in. Take them to yourself, but do not stop there. These are tales for passing on.

JAN ANDREWS

THE FOREST BRIDE

ONCE upon a time there was a man who had come across the ocean from Finland to work in the lumber trade. He went to the forests on the edge of Lake Superior. With him he brought his wife and his three sons. He settled in a village by the lake's great waters, leaving his family in their small house during the winter months while he went off to some far logging camp.

His new life was good, but he was also a man who liked to keep to the old ways. When his sons were almost grown, he called them to him. He said he had decided that it was time for each one of them to go and find a bride. The sons were willing enough, but they did not know how to begin.

"You must do as we used to do in the Old Country," their father told them. "You must take an ax and go to the edge of the forest. Each one of you must cut down a tree and follow the direction that it points."

The sons agreed, and the next morning they set out. The oldest brother was the first to swing the ax, of course. As his tree came tumbling to the ground, he saw that it was pointing west. He was delighted, for he knew all he had to do was go to the next village. On a farm just outside the village, there lived a girl. He had seen her at a dance once, and he had thought about her often since.

Then came the second son's turn. His tree pointed east. His eyes shone, for he knew that two villages away in that direction there was a blacksmith. The blacksmith had a daughter. When the second son had met her, he had thought how pretty she looked.

The youngest son went last. His name was Veiko. His tree pointed straight into the forest. His brothers laughed and laughed.

"So," they said to him, "who are you going to marry? Some little fox with pointed ears? Some slow old beaver?"

Veiko said he did not know, but he was certain his father's advice was good and useful. He set off at once and walked for a long time. He had almost given up when, through the trees, he saw a clearing filled with sunlight.

In the clearing there was a cabin. It was small and it did not look prosperous but he knocked politely. When no one answered, he pushed on the door and went in. His spirits sank, for all he could see was a square table, and on that table a small brown mouse.

"What am I going to do now?" he said to himself.

To his amazement, the mouse sat up on her haunches and prinked her whiskers.

"What is the matter?" she asked. "Why are you sighing? Can I help?"

Veiko could see no reason not to answer. "I am looking for a bride," he said, and he told the mouse about his father's instructions and about how his brothers had laughed.

The mouse prinked her whiskers one more time. "I would be your sweetheart, your bride."

"You?" said Veiko.

"Yes," she answered. "And you need not worry. I will be as loyal and faithful and true as any bride might be."

When Veiko looked at her now, he thought what a dear little thing she was.

"Be my bride then," he said.

The mouse was so pleased that she began to sing. Veiko listened spellbound, for it seemed to him the sound was the sweetest in all the world.

"I must go home and tell my father," he said to her. "But, of course, I will come back."

Off he went at a run. His brothers were home already. His oldest brother was saying how pleased the girl on the farm had been to see him and how, yes, she would marry him. His second brother was saying how the blacksmith's daughter had been more than happy, too.

"And you?" they said to Veiko, when they had finished talking. "You? What did you find?"

Veiko drew himself up. "I found a fine lady," he answered. "She is dressed all in velvet, and when she sings I am happier than I have been in all my life."

Their father was pleased. "This is a good beginning," he said to them. "But now I must make certain these sweethearts that you have chosen will make good wives for you."

He said that his sons must go back and put their brides to the test to be sure that they could cook. That was how it was in those days. Men and women had separate tasks to do within the household, and there was no changing this.

"Bring me a loaf of bread that each has baked," the father said.

The first son set off swiftly. A farmer's daughter? He was sure she knew everything about baking bread. The second son was no less eager. Had he not seen the blacksmith's daughter wiping flour from her hands when he had arrived?

With Veiko it was another matter. In fact, by the time he reached the door of the cabin, his head was hanging down and he was sighing once again. The little mouse did not notice this at first. She was just so glad to see him. She ran around and around the table top. She sang again for joy. It was only then that she realized that Veiko was still standing in the doorway. He had not taken a step toward her.

"Are you not pleased to see me?" she asked.

"Oh, yes, of course," Veiko answered. "But my father has set a test for you."

"Do you think I cannot do what is required of me?" the mouse said.

Veiko shrugged. "My father has told me I must bring him a loaf of bread that you have baked."

"Bread!" said the mouse. "Bread is nothing."

Veiko saw now that there was a little silver bell on the table. The mouse picked it up; she rang it. Veiko heard a rustling and a scampering all around. Mice appeared from every crack and corner, far more mice than he could count.

"Go," his mouse commanded them. "Bring me—each of you—a grain of the finest wheat."

The mice ran off quickly but it seemed to Veiko that he had scarcely blinked and they were back. Each had brought a grain of wheat, too, just as his mouse had ordered. In a twinkling the grains were piled together. They were ground and turned into flour. Soon a wonderful loaf of white wheat bread stood ready.

Veiko thanked his mouse over and over. Bidding goodbye, he took the loaf and started home.

As before, his brothers had arrived ahead of him. His oldest brother had placed a loaf of dark rye bread before his father.

"Rye bread is good for folks such as us," his father said.

The second son produced a loaf made with oat flour and potatoes.

"That is good, too," his father agreed.

Now it was Veiko's turn. He put the wheat loaf before them.

"Wheat bread!" said his father. "No one has white wheat bread. It must be true then that your sweetheart is a person of wealth."

"Did he not say she was a fine lady?" his brothers joked.

"I did," said Veiko.

"And how does a fine lady make bread? Tell us that," his brothers demanded.

"She rings a little bell," said Veiko. "She calls her servants to help her."

"Food is one thing," said his father. "But I must know your wives can keep you clothed as well. Go and tell them they must each weave a piece of cloth."

This, too, was as before. The first brother could not wait to leave, for he had seen the loom in his sweetheart's kitchen. The second brother also went quickly. He was certain his bride would succeed. But Veiko—poor Veiko. A loaf of bread was one thing; a piece of woven cloth was something else.

Again when he went into the cabin, his head was hanging low. Again the little mouse was so glad to see him. She ran around on the table and sang her sweet song. Then, of course, she saw Veiko's face.

"Was your father not happy with the bread I baked for you?" she demanded.

"Oh, yes," said Veiko. "He was very happy indeed."

"So what is the matter?"

"He wants you to weave a piece of cloth."

"Cloth is no more difficult than bread," said the mouse.

Once more she took the little bell into her paws. Once more she rang it. Once more there was a rustling and a scampering all around. This time, however, she ordered each mouse to bring her a stalk of flax.

Again the mice ran off. Again they returned before Veiko had scarcely blinked. They worked then, preparing the flax and spinning it and carding it. When that was done, Veiko's mouse wove for him a large piece of linen so fine that it could be folded and fitted into a walnut shell.

Veiko thanked the mouse and said he would return to her. He put the walnut shell in his pocket and set out.

His oldest brother had a square of fabric woven of rough wool.

"It will do," said his father.

His second brother had fabric made from wool that was not so coarse.

"That is better," said his father.

They looked then at Veiko. "And what about you?"

When Veiko brought out the walnut shell, his brothers roared with laughter. "A fine lady indeed," they teased him. "So fine, she does not even know what weaving is."

Veiko opened the walnut shell. He took out the linen and unfolded it. His father fingered the fabric.

"It is so soft," he said.

"And how did she make it—this fine lady of yours?" his brothers asked.

"She rang her bell," answered Veiko. "She sent her servants from her. She had them bring flax to prepare and spin and card for her, and then she did the work."

"It is enough," said his father. "I am sure now that all of you will be well married. Go to your brides and bring them here to your home."

Veiko's heart sank lower than it had ever done before. He could almost hear his brothers' mockery. He imagined his father's disappointment. Still, once more, he set out. As he walked through the forest, he thought about the little mouse.

She had been loyal and faithful and true to him, just as she had promised. She was always so pleased to see him. She had done everything he asked, even when he doubted her. And there was her song.

By the time he reached the sunlit clearing, he had decided that he would take her home with pride.

This time, then, they were glad to see each other. The little mouse was even more excited when Veiko told her that now she was to come to his home.

"I must go in style," she declared at once, and again she rang her bell.

She summoned for herself a coach that was made out of a walnut shell. It had six gray mice to pull it. It had a white mouse with a golden feather in its hat to sit in the front as the coachman, and a white mouse in a jacket with gold buttons to go behind as the footman.

Veiko laughed with delight. As they made their way back, he talked to the little mouse, telling her how he would look after her and how, when they met his father, she need not be scared.

All went well until they came to the bridge that crossed the river at the edge of the village. Just as they were setting out on it, Veiko saw a man he knew coming from the other direction. They met at the middle of the bridge. The man greeted Veiko, but then his eye fell on Veiko's companions.

"Mice!" he cried out. "There is only one place for mice."

Before Veiko could protest, the man lifted his foot. He gave a great kick, and the little mouse and the carriage and the mice to pull it and the coachman mouse and the footman mouse were swept off the bridge and down into the depths below. The man went on his way, but Veiko stood there gazing into the river. As he saw the water swirling past him, carrying the little mouse away from him, he knew how truly he loved her. Tears poured down his cheeks. He felt as if his heart would break.

Who knows how long he would have stayed there grieving if he had not heard the sound of something happening farther down the river's bank. Looking up, he saw a splendid carriage coming out of the water. The carriage was pulled by six gray horses. At the front there was a coachman with a golden feather in his hat; at the back there was a footman wearing a jacket with gold buttons. Leaning from the window was a young woman. To Veiko, she seemed a very fine lady indeed.

"Will you come and ride with me?" she called out to him.

"I cannot ride with you. You are too grand for me. I am the son of a logger. You are too beautiful," Veiko said.

"You loved me when I was a mouse. Can you not love me now?"

Veiko stepped from the bridge. The carriage came closer.

"Was it really you?" he asked.

The young woman nodded. She sang a little. Then he was certain.

"How could this be?" he said.

"I was under an enchantment," she told him. "I had to remain a mouse until someone should agree to marry me and someone else should push me into the river to drown me."

"Do you still wish to be my bride?" Veiko asked her.

"Of course!" she cried. "Of course!"

They looked into each other's eyes with joy. Veiko climbed into the carriage. He rode at his sweetheart's side.

Before long a wedding was held. All three brothers and their brides were married. Veiko's brothers were envious of him, but Veiko's father said that each of his sons had made a good choice. He said the old ways were the best even in a new country.

Veiko just smiled. He did not stay long in the village. He went to his bride's home in a large city by another Great Lake. Her family were people of wealth. Through them and through his own endeavors, Veiko grew wealthy, too.

For all his riches, he never lost his kindness and his humbleness of heart. Nor did his wife, his sweetheart. In the end, the two of them became famous, but it was not for grand living. Their fame was for the doing of good deeds. They lived in joy and contentment.

There is only one more thing to tell about them. Sometimes, when they were alone in the evenings, they would go down to the kitchen. They would call to the mice and invite them to come out from their hiding places to run around and play.

MARIA'S GIFT

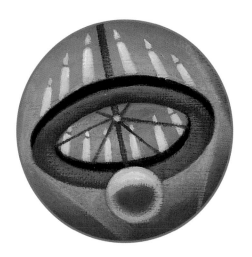

How far is it from a rugged island in Greece to a coal-mining village in the Rocky Mountains? Farther than Maria could have imagined. More carts and boats and ships and trains and wagons and weeks of traveling than she could ever have dreamed.

And why had they made the journey? Maria did not know the answer. She knew that in Greece they had been poor. She knew her father had said they must leave to find their fortune, but it seemed to her that if the family was better off at all, it was by little indeed.

Maria's mother had died on the journey. Now Maria was the mother to her brothers and sisters in their small shack. Each day she made her father's breakfast and a lunch for him to carry. She watched him set out with the other men toward the mine. Then she busied herself, doing what she could to raise the young ones.

She cooked and cleaned. She stitched and tended. Her life was hard. Somehow, however, she was not unhappy, for the mountains seemed to welcome her and she loved them. In summer, whenever there was some time with no work to be done, she would take the children to the high meadows and wander with them by the streams. In winter she would go outside and gaze toward the peaks.

As well she had her father's stories—the ones he told faithfully each evening no matter how tired he was from toiling with shovel and pick. They were the stories he had brought with him, and they made everyone feel better.

"You see!" he would say when the stories were finished. "There are such things as happy endings."

One day, Maria heard the shrilling of the whistle that told everyone in the village there had been an accident at the mine. Rocks had fallen.

Maria went as all did to wait at the mine entrance. She saw her father's body among the others, carried on stretchers through the gates.

What was she to do? Now that her father was dead there would be no money. The family would have nowhere to live and nothing to eat.

Day after day Maria went from door to door, but no one would hire her. Finally she found a place in the home of the mine owner.

The hours were long and the wages were low. At the end of the week Maria had only enough to pay the rent. Each day, then, she waited till the evening to mix the dough for the next day's bread. When the mixing was done, she left with the remnants of the dough still sticking to her fingers. At home she soaked the dough in water to make a kind of porridge to feed her brothers and sisters and herself.

So it went on. The strange thing was that while the children of the mine owner and his wife were thin and pale and weak and cranky, Maria's brothers and sisters were as strong and healthy, as rosy-cheeked and cheerful as anyone could wish.

One day the mine owner's wife noticed this as they were playing in the street. In her amazement, she went to consult her friends.

"You should see if the girl takes anything from you. Perhaps she is stealing," the friends told her.

The mine owner's wife kept watch. She saw the dough that went out of the house every day on Maria's fingers. When she mentioned this, her friends were all in agreement.

"With the dough she is stealing your children's luck," they said.

The mine owner's wife called Maria to her the next morning. She told Maria that from now on she was to clean off every scrap of dough before she left. Maria begged, she pleaded. The mine owner's wife would show no mercy. Indeed, that evening she sent Maria to wash her hands over and over. She inspected Maria's fingers to make sure that there was not a single speck of dough left on them.

When Maria's brothers and sisters greeted her, she had nothing to give them. They were so hungry they began to cry. Maria wept as well, but not for long. Pulling her shawl over her head, she went begging until she was given a few dry crusts.

When the crusts had been eaten, she put the children to bed and watched them fall asleep. She knew that although begging might do for one day, it would not do for another. She could not bear to watch the children starve. In despair, just at midnight, she went out into the darkness and began to walk.

As she followed the rough road that led out of the village, she saw a light shining in the hills above her. She started to climb toward it. The light was coming from a tent.

Maria went inside. In the middle of the tent there was a wonderful candelabra with twelve candles. Dangling from the center of the candelabra was a golden ball.

As well there were twelve young men seated in a circle. To the right of the entrance sat one who had his snow boots unbuckled. Next to him sat one who had his jacket open, and next to him one who was in his shirt sleeves. Each held something in his hands. One had a new green shoot that he was cradling, one a small bunch of crocus flowers, one a newborn calf.

Next to them sat three young men whose skins were bronzed from the sun. They wore wide-brimmed hats. They were bare-chested. They held the flowers of summer—daisies, lupins and clover. All had baskets of berries and early vegetables and hay stalks on their laps.

Beside them were three clothed for the time when the frosts come at night. One had a scythe and a sickle, a bundle of corn and a sheaf of ripe, gold wheat. One had his arms full of squash and pumpkins. The last was wearing a heavy jacket, but he had a gun and a pair of downed geese in his hands.

And next to them? Those young men were bundled up in furs and sheepskins. The ear flaps of their hats were pulled down low, and their collars were pulled up high. One had skis beside him and one snowshoes. One had a trapper's tools.

All the men welcomed Maria as if they had been expecting her, and they invited her to sit a while. They asked her how she had come and why. She told them of her troubles.

The young man who was closest to her on the left—the last of the ones dressed for winter—at once got to his feet. He had a limp, but he set a table before her and covered it with food and drink. When she had eaten her fill, one of the young men asked her to tell them what she thought about the months of the year.

"Tell us of March and April and May especially," the first young man said.

"They are good months," Maria replied at once. "By March we notice that the days are longer. We know that spring is coming. As the ice melts, there are puddles. We find flowers. By May the tracks in the hills are easier to walk on. People can work in their gardens, getting them ready for planting. As the snow leaves the mountain tops, water flows down. The rivers are full and the fish swim freely."

"You like those months, then?"

Maria nodded.

"What about June, July and August?" one of the next three young men asked.

"Those are the best months for the poor," she answered. "They are the season when it does not matter that our clothes are thin. We need no oil for the lamps because the daylight lasts so long. Food is more plentiful. Storms bring rain. The cattle fatten. Sometimes there is even milk."

"And September, October and November?" the next young men put in.

"It begins to be cold once more, but there has been the harvest. Supplies come from the farms. The elk and the sheep come down from the high places. People are joyous. They look forward to the holiday time to come."

"And now," asked the last three, "what about December and January and February? What do you think of them?"

"It is true," said Maria, "that those are the months when life is hardest—the months when some must die. But if we did not have those months, when would my brothers and my sisters be able to go sliding? How would the plants have time to rest? When would there be the long inside evenings when we can sit together, talking and singing songs?"

"You would not change the months? Not one of them?"

"No," said Maria. "I would not."

The young man who had been holding the wheat sheaf put it down beside him. He left the tent and came back carrying a great stoppered jar.

"Take it with you," he said to her. "But do not open it until you are home once more."

By dawn, as the miners were setting out for work, Maria stood again on her own doorstep. She went first to check on her brothers and sisters, although she did not wake them. When she was certain they were safe, she found a cloth and spread it on the floor. She opened the jar and turned it up to empty it. A stream of gold coins poured out.

Picking up just one gold coin, she ran out to the store. She bought bread and butter, eggs and cheese. As she was returning, she met the mine owner. He asked her what she was doing and she could see no reason not to tell him, for she was so delighted with her luck.

When the mine owner went home from work that day, he told his wife, and her eyes lit up at the thought of all that wealth.

She, too, set out at midnight. She, too, came to the tent with its wonderful candelabra. She entered and saw the twelve young men. She was welcomed and asked why she had come. She said she was poor and so they fed her. Then they asked her about the months.

"Each one is worse than the one before," she told them. "The summers are so hot, you'd think the skin would burn from our bones. Rain may come but it is hardly even enough to settle the dust. There is all that trouble of canning what has grown in the gardens. There is all that cooking. By November we are exhausted. There is no end to the work, though. I must have someone to carry in wood and coal for the fireplace. It is so cold that we can scarcely go outside. December and January are bad enough, but the worst of all is that Lame John of a February. That is when the temperatures sink the lowest. Maybe we could get used to it but, of course, we do not have the chance. March comes and April. Everything is sodden from snow melt. My children all have coughs and colds. They've hardly even recovered and the light begins to be blinding. The sun is beating on us once again."

"So there is not one month you can get on with?" the young men asked her.

"Not one," she told them. "Indeed, I would be rid of them all, if I could."

The young men turned to the one with the wheat sheaf. He went out and came in carrying a stoppered jar. The mine owner's wife took it eagerly, but she was careful to remember the instructions not to remove the stopper until she was home.

When she came to her house, she did not check on her children. She did not even tell her husband. She simply emptied the jar as quickly as she could. From it there came a great thick cloud of coal dust. The dust settled over everything and it settled on her. All her life she tried to wash that dust off, but she never could.

As for Maria, she spent the gold she had been given wisely and generously. She started with a sack of flour so she could bake bread instead of buying it. She planned and figured and finally decided she would open a store of her own.

People came to shop and she was kind to them. She never let anyone go hungry. If a family had no money, she gave them extra time to pay.

Her brothers and sisters grew up and moved to other places, but Maria had no wish to go elsewhere. She kept walking in the mountains and gazing at their peaks.

She gathered the children of the village together and told them stories. They came to listen often.

"My father was right," she said to them. "There are such things as happy endings—in the end."

THE FLY

A MAN and his wife left their home in terror. They took their son, Ngoc, and found a boat that would carry them, because they were certain they would soon be killed. They found their way to a camp, but a camp is not a place to live. There are too many people. There is too little food.

How great was their relief when they heard that they had been accepted in North America as refugees! They would have wept for joy but for one thing. The man's brother was in the camp as well. He and his wife had filled out the same papers for themselves and their two small children, but their application had been refused.

For a while the man and his wife wondered how they would ever be able to leave their only surviving relatives behind. At last they decided they would make a promise first.

The day before their departure, the man went to his brother and said, "When we reach the new land, we will do whatever we can to help you. We will find a way to bring you to be with us, and we will send you as much as we can spare."

Ngoc and his parents set out. Once they arrived, their promise was not forgotten. They went to a big city where they thought they might find work. As soon as they had even begun to be settled, the man started to send his brother money.

Life was hard for the man and his wife. In Vietnam he had been the owner of a successful business. Now he had to work for others, taking the first job he could find. His wife had sold beautiful clothes, but she could not do that any longer.

The new land seemed so strange to them.

As they watched their son, Ngoc, they thought that perhaps for him it was easier. He had help from his teacher in school. He learned English quickly. He seemed to understand better what was needed. Sometimes his confidence puzzled them. Sometimes they felt hurt, because he seemed to be leaving them behind.

The weeks turned into months and a letter came from the man's brother saying that one of his children was sick. The family was thankful for what the man had sent to them already, but they had to have more money for medicine or the little girl would die.

"Life gets worse here every day," the brother wrote.

The man sent money at once, but it was more than he and his wife could afford. When the time came to pay the rent, they did not have enough. The landlord showed no sympathy. He was a person who took much and gave little.

The man did his best to explain, but it was Ngoc's pleading that finally convinced the landlord to wait. Ngoc had to plead once more the next month when the man had to send more money to his brother and there was not enough for the rent again.

This time, however, the landlord had a plan. He made the man sign a piece of paper agreeing to pay a heavy sum of interest. The man had a feeling this was not right but it was winter and he was in a country whose ways he did not yet understand. He was desperate to make sure he and his family were not evicted.

Word came that the child of the man's brother was better.

"You saved her life," the letter said.

The man was happy for his niece, but he grew more and more despairing for himself. He could pay the rent each month now but, because of the interest, the debt for the two missed months was increasing by the day. He and his wife did all they could to budget more carefully and to save a little, but there was no catching up.

The landlord waited. He let the few hundreds that had been owed turn into thousands. At the end of a year, he appeared on the man's doorstep. He said that this time, if he was not paid in full by the next morning, he would throw the family out at once.

"Where will we go?" the man demanded.

"That is no concern of mine," the landlord said.

The man would have given up, but Ngoc was determined.

"My teacher would not agree," he insisted. "She would say that this is wrong."

In the morning Ngoc got up early. His father had planned to stay home to meet the landlord.

"No," Ngoc said. "I will meet him. If you and Mother lose your jobs, that will help no one."

Sadly and reluctantly, the man and his wife set off for work. As they went, the man thought of how—in Vietnam—things had been so different. He had known what to say. He had been the family's protector.

Ngoc did not have to wait long.

"My parents have gone to work," he told the landlord. "They left me no money because they have none. But if they do not keep working, how can they ever pay?"

"You must tell me what their jobs are," the landlord demanded. He wanted to know so that he could go to where the man and his wife worked and have the money owed to him taken directly from their salaries.

Ngoc was suspicious. He pretended he was thinking very hard.

"I cannot say," he burst out.

"Why not?" the landlord asked.

"Because I do not know."

"How can you not know?"

"You have seen how it is with my parents. The words for their jobs are too difficult for them to manage. My mother tells me she turns night into day."

"And your father?"

"He tells me he turns rags into riches."

"It is enough," said the landlord. "I shall figure it out."

The next morning he was back on the doorstep. He had spent the whole night without sleeping, trying to imagine what "night into day" and "rags into riches" might mean.

Ngoc merely repeated what he had said already.

"What else can I do?" he cried.

The landlord went away again, but by then he was angry. Not only did he want his money. He could not bear it that Ngoc was getting the better of him—a boy, an immigrant! He spent another night tossing and turning. He raved and ranted to himself. He came back one more time. He threatened and pleaded.

"My mother turns night into day. My father turns rags into riches."

The answer was always the same. Suddenly a smile came to the landlord's face for it occurred to him that he could find out what he needed through a trick.

"Listen," he said. "I am sorry. I have been selfish and thoughtless. I would like to make amends. I want to go to your parents myself at this very moment and tell them everything is forgiven. They do not have to pay me anything at all."

"If only I knew how to help you!" Ngoc groaned. "My parents would be so pleased. But I do not even have the addresses."

The landlord acted as if he had an idea. "Why not go to your teacher and ask her? I am sure your teacher will know."

Ngoc pretended to be eager.

There was the landlord then—the next morning—on the doorstep even earlier. Ngoc hesitated.

"What is the matter?" the landlord asked.

"I am afraid you are not going to forgive my parents' debt. Not really."

"You doubt my word?"

"But..." Ngoc tried to look bewildered. "But, where we come from, a promise is always given with an oath."

"An oath? An oath is not necessary here."

"I cannot believe you without an oath."

The landlord was growing ever more impatient. "All right," he said. "If you insist, then I will swear an oath."

"And an oath must have a witness," said Ngoc.

"A witness?"

With that, a fly came through the door and landed on the wall.

"What would a boy such as this really know of witnesses?" the landlord thought to himself.

He pointed in the fly's direction.

"What about the fly?" he suggested. "Could that be a witness?"

Ngoc looked delighted. "Oh, yes! A fly would be perfect," he agreed.

The landlord spoke solemnly. "As the fly is my witness, if you will tell me where your parents work, I will gladly go to them and forgive their debt to me," he proclaimed.

"This is what my teacher says," Ngoc answered. "She says my mother turns night into day because she works at the lighting factory. My father turns rags into riches because he works in the place where they cut old clothes into pieces and sell them. The pieces are bought in bundles. They are used for cleaning."

The landlord went off laughing.

Since he needed an order from the court to take the salaries of Ngoc's parents, they were called to appear before a judge. The man showed his son the piece of paper on which all this was written.

"Now we will lose everything," he said.

"I will come with you," Ngoc declared.

In the court, as soon as the judge began to speak of the debt, Ngoc jumped to his feet.

"The landlord said the debt was to be over. He swore an oath to me."

The judge would have called for quiet, but the landlord was already answering. "I did not. I did no such thing."

The judge turned to Ngoc. "Tell me what you know," he asked.

"I know the landlord came to my home. He said that if I would tell him where my parents worked—"

"I didn't even talk to the boy. Why would I?" the landlord interrupted.

"Do you have any proof? Something in writing?" the judge asked.

"I have nothing in writing, but I do have a witness," said Ngoc.

The judge looked interested. "A witness? Tell me who he is and I will send for him."

Ngoc reached into his pocket.

"I have brought the witness with me. I have it in a jar."

"A witness cannot be in a jar."

"Yes, it can. It's a fly. "

"You see!" said the landlord. "The boy knows nothing. How can he say whether I spoke to him or whether I did not?"

"I'm afraid," said the judge, "a fly cannot be a witness."

"But the landlord said it could," answered Ngoc.

"When did he say it?" demanded the judge.

"He said it when the fly was sitting on his nose."

Troubled as they were, even Ngoc's parents could not help but laugh at the thought of this.

"The fly was not on my nose," the landlord burst out. "It came through the door. It landed on the wall."

"And when was this?" the judge asked.

"When I was trying to get this boy to—"

"Ah!" said the judge. "So you did speak to the boy? You spoke to him after all."

The landlord grew flustered. "I only spoke to him a little."

"You spoke to him and you said you didn't. To lie to the court is a serious matter. Now you must tell me everything that happened."

When the judge heard about the interest, he called the landlord an exploiter. He said he should be ashamed.

"These people were trying to help others in situations such as we can hardly imagine," he declared.

He asked if there was anything the family could pay. The man, his wife and Ngoc talked together.

"My father says if they could pay a little each week...and just for the original debt..." Ngoc interpreted.

The judge turned to the landlord. "That is what I am ordering. That and no more."

Because of his lie, the landlord could not argue. He went away unhappy, but there was nothing he could do.

That night the man and his wife told their son how grateful they were to him. They also made another promise. They promised that no matter how difficult it might seem to them, they would study until their English was as good as his.

They paid their debt and moved soon afterwards. When they moved, they made certain they had a better landlord.

The man's brother and his family never came to join them, but they did go to another country where they did not need help any more.

The man did not have to go on turning rags into riches forever, nor did his wife keep turning night into day. As their English improved, so did their circumstances.

Ngoc grew up to be a fine and generous citizen. In time he became a lawyer. He spent his days helping new immigrants such as he and his parents had once been.

"I turn new immigrants into old," he said.

THE PINCOYA'S CHILD

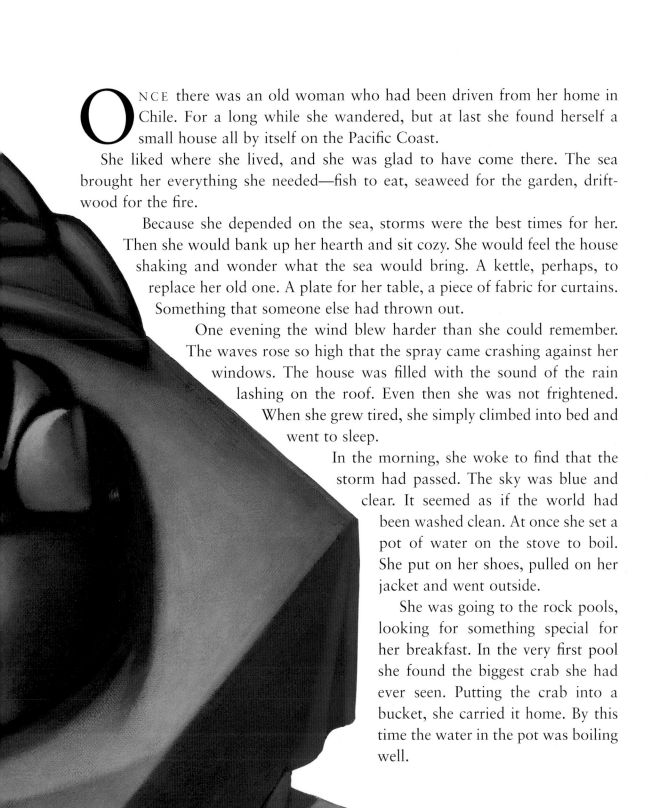

O N C E there was an old woman who had been driven from her home in Chile. For a long while she wandered, but at last she found herself a small house all by itself on the Pacific Coast.

She liked where she lived, and she was glad to have come there. The sea brought her everything she needed—fish to eat, seaweed for the garden, driftwood for the fire.

Because she depended on the sea, storms were the best times for her. Then she would bank up her hearth and sit cozy. She would feel the house shaking and wonder what the sea would bring. A kettle, perhaps, to replace her old one. A plate for her table, a piece of fabric for curtains. Something that someone else had thrown out.

One evening the wind blew harder than she could remember. The waves rose so high that the spray came crashing against her windows. The house was filled with the sound of the rain lashing on the roof. Even then she was not frightened. When she grew tired, she simply climbed into bed and went to sleep.

In the morning, she woke to find that the storm had passed. The sky was blue and clear. It seemed as if the world had been washed clean. At once she set a pot of water on the stove to boil. She put on her shoes, pulled on her jacket and went outside.

She was going to the rock pools, looking for something special for her breakfast. In the very first pool she found the biggest crab she had ever seen. Putting the crab into a bucket, she carried it home. By this time the water in the pot was boiling well.

The old woman set the crab on the table. When she looked at it, she saw that the pot was not nearly big enough to hold such a creature, so she went outside once more to find herself a stone. Using the stone as a hammer, she split the crab's shell into two pieces.

Once the shell was split, she saw inside—not crab meat—but a tiny child.

The little girl was perfect in every way, except that where another child would have had legs there was the tail of a fish. The old woman reached out her hands and the child reached toward her. The old woman noticed that the hair on the child's head was dark, dark red.

She looked into the little girl's eyes and saw how gray they were. Their color filled her with the memory of standing by the water looking out on a calm, soft day in the country where she had grown up.

The old woman knew what the child was. She was the child of a pincoya. The old woman had heard about the pincoya when she was little. She knew they were always out there in the sea.

But surely, the old woman thought, the child must be hungry. She took the pot off the stove and brought some leftover soup to heat instead. When the soup was warm, she took the child in her arms and fed her. She played with the little girl's small fingers. She tickled her to make her laugh.

The old woman spent all day with the child, talking to her and caring for her, singing her to sleep when she thought she was tired. By the end of the day, she knew just how much she wanted to keep the little girl with her.

Night came once more. All through it, the old woman worried and fretted and tossed and turned.

By morning she was certain she needed someone else to help her decide what to do. At first she could think of no one. Then she remembered that in a village on her journey she had met an even older woman who had seemed both wise and kind. That woman had walked with her by the water. She had given her tea and a place to rest.

The old woman wrapped the little girl in a blanket and put her in a basket. Tying the basket on her back, she set out. She walked until she came to the place she was seeking. She found the house and knocked on the door. The older woman made her welcome, although she was surprised to see her.

"Why have you come?" she asked.

The woman from the seashore opened the basket. The other old woman gasped in amazement, but she reached out to touch the child's cheeks.

"How did you find her?" she demanded.

The old woman from the seashore told her the story of the storm and the crab.

"Where I was born, we would say she is a child of the pincoya," she added.

The old woman from the village nodded. They looked at the child's gray eyes.

"Whatever we might call her, we know she is a child of the sea," the older woman declared.

The answer was not the one the old woman from the seashore had wanted. Still, she said thank you for the help she had been given. She sat and ate some of the smoked fish she was offered. She listened to stories of the older woman's family and friends. She put the basket on her back once more and made the long journey home.

In the morning she rose early. She fed the little girl. She talked to her and tickled her. She put her into the basket and set it outside on a rock where the waves could wash up against it.

The child turned her head to look out across the water. The old woman saw how the child's gray eyes shone more brightly.

Leaving the child, she went to sit and wait. As she looked into the bay, she saw something floating on the sea's surface. At first she thought it was seaweed. As it came closer, she realized that it was long, red hair.

She expected the pincoya to take the child at once.

"Will you not keep her?" the pincoya called instead.

The old woman went down to the edge of the water. The pincoya swam nearer.

"She is not mine," the old woman burst out.

"No," said the pincoya. "She is mine, but she is small and weak. I need someone to care for her. If she stays with us, the sea wolves will get her. She is a danger to herself. She is a danger to us."

"I will care for her," said the old woman.

"I will come for her when she is strong enough," the pincoya answered. "In payment, our people will make sure the sea brings extra things to you."

"To have the child is riches enough," the old woman said.

The pincoya swam to the child and talked to her for a moment. Then she swam away. The old woman watched until she could see only the long red hair and then only the sea's surface. She took the child with her into the house.

All that summer, they stayed together. The old woman talked to the child and fed her, sang to her and made her laugh. When they went out to the shore, the old woman put the little girl in the rock pools to swim. And always, as the pincoya had promised, the sea brought everything they needed.

Fall turned into winter and then, at last, to spring. The old woman saw that the rock pools were no longer really big enough to hold the child. But, oh, how much she loved her by then.

The months of summer began to pass. At nights once more she worried and fretted and tossed and turned.

The child was heavier by this time, of course. The old woman needed a much bigger basket to carry her, but the sea had brought one. Again she wrapped the child carefully. Again she set off with her and walked until she came to where the other old woman lived.

"How lovely she is," the old woman from the village cried when the basket was set on the table and the child was lifted out.

"I kept her because I was asked to," the old woman from the seashore said. "It is as I thought. Her mother is a pincoya."

The older woman nodded.

"She was too small for them to keep her."

"And now?"

"Now she is stronger."

The old woman from the village looked at the child's gray eyes one more time. The old woman from the seashore remembered how each time the child looked out over the water, her eyes shone more brightly.

"You will miss her," said the older woman. "You know that it is time, though, don't you?"

The old woman from the seashore nodded. "Whatever we might call her, we know she is a child of the sea," she said.

Once more the woman from the seashore gave thanks for the help she had been given. Once more she ate and listened to the talk of family and friends before she set out.

In the morning, when she and the child had eaten, she put the little girl at the ocean's edge. She sat where she had sat before, and she waited. As the weeks and months had passed, sometimes she had thought she had again seen long red hair floating on the water in the distance. When she saw the hair now, it came closer.

"I thank you for what you have done for us," the pincoya said as she took her little girl in her arms.

"And I thank you. I am grateful for the things you have brought me, but I am far more grateful for the child."

"She can go with us now," said the pincoya. "She is stronger."

The old woman reached toward the little girl. She felt the child's fingers grip her own hands firmly.

"Is there anything else we can do for you?" the pincoya asked.

The old woman let go of the child one last time.

"You might tell me where you come from. You might say whether you swim only here or by the country of my birth."

"We swim wherever we want. We travel near, we travel far. That is why the child must be healthy."

"The country of my birth is a long way south."

"We go where the sea goes. We go there."

"When you do, you could think of me. You could remember that I grew up beside those waters. You could tell the child about it."

"I promise," said the pincoya.

The pincoya and her daughter swam away. The old woman watched the two long masses of hair mingling together as they floated on the sea's surface.

For a while after that she was sometimes sure she saw long red hair in the distance. Then, try as she might, she could not see it any more.

She had lived by herself before and been happy enough. She lived by herself again. She thought of the child and of the pincoya. She thought of the older woman who had helped her.

In times of storm and in times of calm, she took what the sea brought to her. Sometimes she thought it brought more good things than ever. Sometimes she was amazed at how she always had enough.

THE COUPLE'S JOURNEY

THE people of the muskeg, the people who live on the wide and open spaces of the tundra where the Winisk River comes out into Hudson Bay—these people are called the Omushkego. Among them, in far-off times, there lived a girl. From the moment of her birth she was filled with beauty. Hers was not just a beauty of face and form and feature, but of kindness and gentleness and joy in life.

Her parents were dead. In the winters she lived with her grandfather in their small hunting camp. In the summers she went with him to the gathering place where the people set up their tipis together, where they met to talk and celebrate, to fish and hunt for ducks and geese.

The girl was much loved, for it seemed to all who knew her that her presence among them was a gift. In the beginning, of course, her grandfather looked after her. But as she grew up and he grew older, more and more it happened that she took care of him.

The time came when the girls of her age were finding husbands. Many young men approached her—fine strong men who were good hunters. No matter how often they asked her, she always told them that her grandfather needed her and that she could not leave. Some of the young men went to her grandfather to request that he arrange a marriage.

"It is for my granddaughter to choose," he said.

Each year now he grew weaker. Before long the girl had to take over the hunting he had once done for both of them. She had to prepare his food with extra thought. All this she did willingly. She helped him to the special places where the sun was warmest. She sat with him quietly in the evenings and listened to him talk.

One summer, quite soon after they reached the gathering place, he fell ill with a sickness that could not be cured. He called her to him and took her hand.

"Soon I must go away from you," he told her. "But you will not be alone. A stranger to our people will ask you to marry him. You may accept him with gladness. Because of all these long years that you have cared for me, your marriage will be blessed. As you have loved me, so he will love you and you will love him."

The girl knew that a stranger had come to the summer camps the past few years. The other young women said he talked of being from a far distant region where there were hills taller than anyone from those flat lands could even imagine—mountains reaching to the skies. The other young women said he would make a very good husband indeed.

The summer camps were large. The girl had seen him but she had never spoken to him. She had been too busy with her grandfather to think about such things.

Before the summer was out, in the time of the berry picking, her grandfather died. The girl stood by his grave. She felt as if the sun and the moon and the stars had disappeared from the sky.

As she wept, she heard a voice. Turning, she saw the stranger behind her. As he reached out to touch her, she felt comfort. His words brought comfort also, so much so that when they went back to her tipi she invited him to visit for a while.

In the weeks that followed, just as her grandfather had told her, love grew between them. Before the time came for her people to be parting for the winter, the young man asked her if she would marry him, and she answered readily, "Yes." There was a wedding feast. When the feast was over, her husband stood before her.

"Shall we go home?" he asked.

This was the question the girl had been expecting. She agreed, although she had no idea how far away that home in the mountains might be.

"These lands are not my own," her husband said to her. "I do not know the ways of them. I cannot hunt here as I should."

"There are two things I ask of you," the girl said. "I ask that I may keep speaking my own language. I also ask that no matter how far we may travel, you will bring me back to see my home again before I die."

The young man promised without hesitation. He would have promised her anything, he loved her so much.

As the summer camp broke up, people came to say farewell to the girl. They wept at the knowledge that she was going from them, for she would be sorely missed. The young couple waited until freeze-up, when the lakes and marshes were covered with ice and traveling became easier. Having gathered all they needed for the journey, they set off.

Crossing the muskeg took many days. When the couple came to the end of the muskeg, they entered the forests. By then they had left the lands of the Omushkego far behind. They had come to the territory of the Oji-Cree and the Ojibway peoples. Sometimes they were welcomed there and sometimes they were not.

No one knows how long they kept going. Perhaps it was only months, perhaps years.

The forests gave way to brush land and then to prairie. When she saw the unending sea of waving prairie grass before her, the girl let out a laugh. She ran forward eagerly, for she could look into the distance forever as she had done at home.

On the prairie, she saw herd upon herd of hump-backed hairy monsters. She watched the monsters grazing, their breath hanging in a mist about them in the dawn. The creatures seemed to darken the earth, there were so many of them.

As the couple crossed the prairie, a wind blew up behind them, and with the wind came fire. Joining hands, the girl and her husband ran ahead of the flames, but the fire raged ever closer. Just when they thought that they would surely perish, they came to a prairie creek. Jumping into the water, they let the fire leap over them. When the fire had passed, the earth was scorched and blackened.

Always they went west. Always they journeyed on. One morning the girl woke to see clouds hanging far off in the sky. All day she watched those clouds and saw that they did not move.

"How can this be?" she asked her husband.

"We have come to the mountains," he told her. "Those are not clouds, but snow."

The way grew steeper. They began to climb through the foothills. Sometimes it seemed to the girl the foothills were so high that the mountains disappeared. She asked about that, too. Whatever questions she had, her husband answered. He began to teach her about this land he knew so well.

At last they reached the hunting camp of his people, but no one was there.

"They have gone to another hunting place," he decided. "It is how it happens. Probably they will come back, but still, in this land we will make our home."

The years passed and the couple had children. They rejoiced in them and raised them well. Some years the hunting was better than others, but there was always enough. If pain or sickness came to the family, the couple found the herbs that would help. Most important, just as the grandfather had foreseen, they continued to be blessed with a strong love for each other.

The husband did not forget the first part of the promise he had given. He worked hard to learn Cree, which is the language of the Omushkego. Cree became the language of the children.

More years went by. At last, even the youngest child had grown up and left the tipi. The couple's work was done.

The wife was filled with a longing. She wanted to see her own lands again.

"Do you remember what you told me?" she said to her husband.

He looked at her kindly, for he understood. He had watched her gazing eastward, and he had known what she was thinking. But, when he answered, he said they could not manage to return.

"We were young then," he told her. "We could do anything. We are old now. The journey is too far."

His wife tried to put the longing from her, but try as she might, it would not go away. Once more she spoke to her husband of his promise. This time he knew, no matter what perils they might face, no matter how long the journey would take, he must agree.

The wife had one more thing to say, however.

"Whatever might happen to me," she told her husband, "for the sake of our children and of their children, you must return."

So they set off. This time as they crossed the prairie, they heard hooves behind them. The buffalo, the hump-backed hairy monsters, were in stampede. Again the couple joined hands. Again they sought the safety of a creek. They held their breath in terror as buffalo upon buffalo leaped above them. They waited for the silence that told them the stampede had passed.

Often it seemed to them that their journey west had been only yesterday. The land had not changed. The scents they remembered were all around them. The birds and plants, the sunrises and sunsets were the same.

Time went by. Storms came and went. There was rain; there was snow. To the couple, none of this mattered. They knew only that they had reached the place where the trees grew ever more numerous. They were traveling once more through the forests, over the lakes and along the rivers. They were crossing the lands of the Ojibway and the Oji-Cree.

Tears of joy filled the woman's eyes when she first saw the muskeg. She cried for joy again as she and her husband came to a rise of land where they could watch the waves of the great sea that filled the Hudson Bay. Once the tears had passed, her heart soared. She was home, back in the lands where she had been born. She and her husband came to the summer gathering place. Her friends were there to greet her. All rejoiced at her return. The summer passed in hunting and fishing and feasting, just as it always had.

Then, like her grandfather before her, she grew sick. Grieve as her husband might, this, too, was a sickness for which there was no cure. She died, and her body was buried by her grandfather's grave. Her husband watched as the children of her people brought wildflowers to lay beside her. He stood alone as she had stood. Once the funeral was over, he turned and left the lands of the Omushkego forever. He kept this promise also. He started the long journey back to his own home.

The Omushkego say this is a true story. They say it tells of how Cree came to be the language of some of the peoples of the mountains. They say those peoples are the descendants of the girl who journeyed from the Omushkego lands.

WISE FATHER, WISE DAUGHTER

THERE are so many reasons why people leave their home and travel to a new country. Paul arrived in sadness and in anger. He had owned a flourishing barbershop, but the laws of the state where he lived had been rewritten. African Americans like himself were no longer free to live where they wanted or work where they chose. Determined that he would not simply suffer this injustice, he decided to leave.

The journey north by boat was hard, but when he came to a town he liked he decided to settle there. He found himself a place to live, unpacked the tools of his trade and opened a barbershop again.

Paul was not an ordinary barber; he was an excellent one. Before long, people were crossing town because of his talents; they were recommending him to their friends. Some days the barbershop was so busy that the line of waiting customers stretched outside the door.

Paul grew more and more satisfied with what he had managed. He thought of others who had arrived at the same time as he had, or even earlier. He knew he had done better than most.

The trouble began on the day he looked in the mirror and saw his first gray hair. He realized then that a time would come when he would be too old to run his business. He had three daughters, but he did not think the barbershop would support all of them—certainly not later when they had their own families to care for. No, he was sure, the business would never be big enough for that.

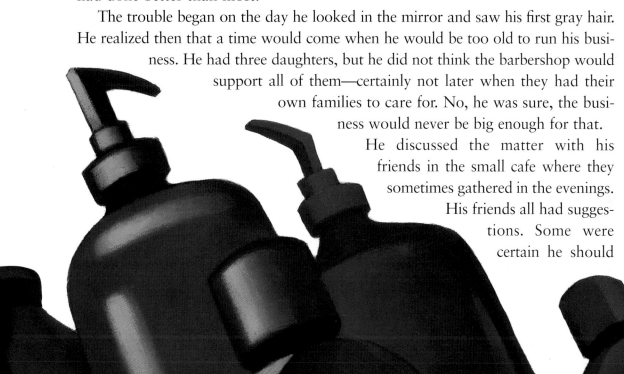

He discussed the matter with his friends in the small cafe where they sometimes gathered in the evenings. His friends all had suggestions. Some were certain he should devise a scheme for dividing the barbershop's customers and having three shops. Others said he should choose the oldest daughter to succeed him. Still others said it should be the one who was the best at a barber's work.

This might have been the best idea, but each of Paul's daughters was as good as the other, for he had trained them all with care. Oh, it was true that one was a little better at keeping the razors at their sharpest, one swept the hairs from the floor more quickly, one cleaned the combs and scissors more often. But they were all of a piece when it came to cutting a customer's hair to just the style that was wanted, shaving a chin so the skin felt as smooth as it should, welcoming people, setting the accounts down in straight columns and adding those columns in a book.

More years went by, and Paul began to worry. He knew he moved around the barbershop more slowly. He could not go to the cafe in the evenings so often, for he was wearier when the work was done. All of his daughters were grown, too. He had said he would give the shop to one of them. He could tell they were waiting. He knew he had to make a choice.

One night he could not even sleep for thinking of it. He got up and went to his window. The moon was full. He dressed and walked up one street and down another. He walked a long way, but by the time he reached home again he thought he could sleep well.

In the morning he called his daughters to him.

"Tomorrow I am going to send you out into the world," he told them. "And I am going to give you each a hundred-dollar bill. Whichever one of you can come back at the end of a year with enough to fill the barbershop in every corner, she will be the one to whom the shop will go."

The next day he placed the money in his daughters' hands. He was sorry to see them leave. Still, he was certain this was the best course.

The oldest daughter had been gone no more than a week before she came back in a new dress and a fine fur coat.

"Why would I want to spend my days toiling as you have done?" she said to him. "I shall make my own way in the world."

Paul was saddened, but now he knew clearly that she was not the one.

His second daughter came a month later. "The task is impossible," she cried out. "I have been thinking and thinking. The only way to succeed in this is to buy a load of dirt."

Knowing that the dirt would ruin the barbershop forever, Paul told her to spend the money as she wanted.

The next month passed, and the next. Nothing happened. Often he would catch himself looking out of the window, checking the calendar, gazing down the street. His youngest daughter did not come.

Finally, the year was almost at an end. Finally, the sun rose on the very last day.

Paul got up. He worked. The hours passed. He was closing the shop when at last his youngest daughter appeared. She had no bags or suitcases, no wagon with her purchases following behind. Still, Paul greeted her and took her inside.

She looked as if she was pleased to be back. He asked her if she would like something to eat or drink. She shook her head. Instead, she put her hand into her pocket. Smiling, she took out a candle and set it on a table. While Paul watched, she struck a match and touched it to the candle's wick.

The candle flame flickered and took hold. The candle light spread from floor to ceiling, filling every corner, just as he had wished.

Paul threw back his head and laughed. The sound of his laughter filled the barbershop as well. He took his daughter in his arms and hugged her. For had not this— his youngest child—shown wisdom? And is not wisdom a light for all the world?

So it was that Paul's youngest daughter became the owner of the business he had built. When he could work no longer, he often came to sit and watch her. He chatted to the customers, for there were always customers waiting in line.

Paul died in time. By then his daughter had made the business even better. By then she was married and had children of her own. Since those days, although they have done many other things as well, there has always been some member of Paul's family in the barbering business. In fact, the next time you go to get your hair cut, you might meet one of them yourself.

LITTLE DAUGHTER OF THE SNOW

THERE was once an old man and an old woman. They had come from Russia soon after they were married, when they were just a young couple. They had bought a piece of land where the prairies become bush and the grasses are replaced by birch and poplar trees. They had cleared it and worked it and, although they were not rich, they had prospered well enough.

They had their crops and they had their cattle. They had chickens, a pig, some cats and a couple of dogs. They might have been completely happy, but they did not have the one thing they longed for above all else. They did not have a child.

They wanted a daughter, especially. Often in the evenings, when all the work was done and they were sitting together, they would talk about her.

"I would teach her to bake bread and milk the cows and knit as I do," the old woman said to her husband.

"I would take her into the fields with me. I would show her when the earth was right for planting and when the wheat was ready to harvest," the old man replied.

"And we would watch her play," the old woman added.

"Oh, yes!" said her husband. "We would love to do that."

Time passed. Then, early one winter, the snow came—not in the small thin shafts that were usual in the region, but in fat, wet flakes that filled the air and almost stuck together by themselves. The old man and the old woman looked out the window and saw that the path to the barn was covered. This was like the snow they knew from Russia, all those years so long ago and far away.

"Do you remember how we used to go out and make ourselves snow people—Baba Yagas, snow witches?" the old woman asked.

"Oh, yes," the old man answered. "We threw snowballs and broke the snow people to pieces just so we could build them up once more."

"What if we make ourselves a little snow daughter?" the old woman suggested.

They put on their coats and went outside. They took the snow in their hands and shaped it. They rolled and molded and patted to make the little snow girl's body, her head, her legs, her arms.

At last, toward evening, the task was finished. There was the snow girl standing before them. She was beautiful, except that her lips were cold and white and unmoving, and her eyes were blind.

Now the fact that they had no real child seemed even more terrible to them.

"Please," said the old man. "Speak to us."

"Please," said the old woman. "Smile."

And the snow girl did smile. Her lips grew rosy red. Her eyes opened. She looked at the old man and the old woman and her face lit up. Before they knew it, she was whirling and dancing around them. As she danced, she sang this song:

No warm blood in me doth glow,
Water in my veins doth flow;
Yet I will laugh and sing and play
By frosty night and frosty day—
Little daughter of the snow.

But whenever I do know
That you love me little, then
I shall melt away again.
Back into the sky I'll go
Little daughter of the snow.

The song made the old man and the old woman smile.

"How could we love you little?" the old man asked her.

"How is it," said the old woman, "that you would not be our more than precious joy?"

Deciding they must get clothes for her to wear, they took her inside. The little daughter of the snow went through the porch and into the kitchen, but when they showed her a seat by the stove, she shook her head.

"Too hot! Too hot!" she cried.

The old woman had the clothes all ready. She had stitched them herself, putting a hope and a wish into each pass of her needle. She had folded them and put them into a closet, and now she brought them out. There was a coat of cloth and a dress with embroidery to go under it; there was a hat of fur and woolen mittens. The old man had made a pair of calfskin boots.

The little daughter of the snow admired her clothes, but she did not want to stay in the kitchen. As soon as she was dressed, she was off into the yard once more.

"It is time for you to be sleeping," the old woman called after her. But the snow girl only laughed.

For a long time, the old man and the old woman watched her dancing and whirling, spreading her arms and singing. When they grew tired, they tried again to get her to come in to them, but she would not do it. Finally, they decided they must go to bed themselves.

In the morning, before their eyes had scarcely opened, they were at the window. How glad they were to see the snow child there. The old woman went out to milk the cows, and the man went to feed the chickens and the pig. When they came back, the little daughter of the snow came to the door with them. When they said she should have breakfast, she showed them how to crush icicles to make ice porridge in a bowl. She would eat nothing else. The ice porridge was hardly gone before she was dancing once again.

So it was, day after day. The old man and the old woman could not have been happier. The little daughter of the snow stayed outside almost all the time, but they did not mind. They loved to watch her dance and they loved to listen, for her laughter and her singing seemed to fill the air. She followed them at their chores and she played and played as they had dreamed.

Sometimes they worried that she had no other children to play with, but there was nothing they could do. There were no other farms or children close at hand. The little daughter of the snow did not seem to be troubled. She played with the dogs and the cats and even the chickens, and she was quite content. When she danced, the hearts of the old man and the old woman danced with her.

"I told her, didn't I?" said the old woman. "I said that she would be our more than precious joy."

The winter was long and cold, as winters in that region are. Still, at last the days grew warmer. The snow began to melt. Patches of bare earth appeared in the fields. Before, the little daughter of the snow had stayed close to the house and the farmyard. Now she ventured farther, exploring the brush land and the bluffs.

A day came when the sun shone so brightly and the sky was so blue, she could not resist. She just kept going, running to see how the buds were swelling, listening to the bird songs on the wind. Twilight caught her and she grew frightened, for when she turned and looked about her, she realized that she did not know her way home.

She found a tree that was older and stronger than the others. She thought that perhaps if she climbed into its branches, she would be high enough to see. Climb as she might, it made no difference. She could find no path.

Twilight turned to darkness. With the darkness she grew so frightened that she began to cry. An old bear that was waking up from its winter sleep came by the tree. It was thin and shaggy, but it stopped.

"Why do you cry?" it called up.

"What else can I do?" she answered. "I am lost. I do not know how to get home."

"I could take you. I could carry you on my back," the old bear offered.

The little daughter of the snow looked down at the bear's great shape.

"I am afraid you might eat me," she answered.

The old bear scratched itself against the tree trunk for a while and went away.

The little daughter of the snow cried even more. A coyote, out for its night of traveling, happened upon her.

"Why do you cry?" it called up.

"What else can I do?" she answered once more. "What else, when I am lost?"

"You could walk by my side," said the coyote. "You could get home that way."

The little daughter of the snow peered down through the darkness. The coyote was not as big as the bear, but it was big enough.

"You might eat me," she called.

The coyote circled the tree a couple of times but soon it, too, was gone.

The little daughter of the snow started to sob. A red fox was the next to hear her.

"Why do you cry?" it asked her.

"Because I am lost," she answered.

"Climb down to the ground," the red fox told her. "Take hold of the ruff of fur behind my head. I'll lead you. You'll be home soon enough."

When the little daughter of the snow looked down, she saw only a slight, thin wisp—hardly more than a shadow. She was on the ground in an instant. She put out her hand and held onto the fox's ruff. The fox went quickly, true to its promise.

They hardly seemed to have gone any distance when the little daughter of the snow could see the light from the old man and the old woman's house.

"Are the dogs tied?" the red fox asked her. "Dogs are dangerous for foxes."

"Always at night," the little daughter of the snow replied.

The red fox led her on. The old man and the old woman were standing on the doorstep. They had searched and searched for her. They were crying themselves, for they were sure that she was dead.

"Here I am," she called out to them. "I've come back to you. I've come back safe and sound."

They took her in their arms. They hugged her and hugged her. Of course, they wanted to know what had happened. She told them about being lost in the brush land. She pointed to the small red fox.

"You should thank him," she said. "I would never have got here by myself."

"We do thank you," said the old woman.

"It is a long time since I have eaten," the small red fox replied.

The old woman went inside to the bread box and brought out some stale loaf ends.

"A hen would be a better gift than loaf ends for one who is hungry," the red fox told her.

"Of course, of course," said the old woman.

She and the old man set off for the chicken coop, but when it came to choosing which hen they would take, it was a different matter. This one was too plump, and that one was too healthy. One had feathers just right for stuffing a pillow; one laid so many eggs.

"A hen is too much for a fox," the old woman insisted finally, and the old man at once agreed.

He fetched two sacks. He did put a hen into the first sack, but into the second he put the biggest of the dogs.

The small red fox's eyes shone when it saw there were two sacks instead of one.

"Two hens," it cried out. "You are very generous."

"You brought our little daughter of the snow to us," the old woman replied.

The old man gave the red fox the sack with the hen in it. The red fox was hungry. It opened the sack at once. The hen came fluttering out, and the fox went after it. The fox had gone no more than two paces when the old man opened the second sack as well. The dog sprang forth, barking and howling. The fox ran, terrified. The dog chased it and sent it off into the night.

When the dog came back, the old man and the old woman congratulated themselves on their cleverness. They petted the dog and said it had done well. They chuckled to think of the trick they had played.

Then they looked around for the little daughter of the snow to share the joke with her, but she was nowhere to be seen. All they heard was the sound of her voice. It was coming from the kitchen, where she was singing:

Old ones, old ones, now I know
Less you love me than a hen,
I shall go away again,

Goodbye, ancient ones, goodbye,
Back I go across the sky;
To my motherkin I go —
Little daughter of the snow.

Quick as they could, they rushed inside. Beside the stove there was a small puddle of water and, by the puddle, the snow child's boots and clothes.

"Do not leave us," they cried, because—despite all that—they could still see her bright eyes and they could feel her dancing. They could hear her voice, too.

Old ones, old ones, now I know
Less you love me than a hen,
I shall melt away again,
To my motherkin I go —
Little daughter of the snow.

A cold wind blew in. It filled the room and reached into every corner. Around and around it went. It carried the snow child with it. She faded and faded. With one last sound of her laughter, she was gone.

She did not come back. The old man and the old woman missed her. Often, in the evenings, they wept thinking of her. As long as they lived, they grieved.

All that was long ago. Who knows, then, what might happen if someone took snow in hand to roll and mold and shape a little snow girl now?

TI-JEAN AND THE CALF

TI-JEAN lived in a small village, where the land stretches back from the south shore of the St. Lawrence River and the streams all flow into the river's waters on their journey to the sea.

Ti-Jean was poor. He and his wife had nothing. One day he said to her, "Perhaps if we would simply *seem* to have what others have, our luck would change."

"How could we do such a thing?" his wife asked him.

"Well," said Ti-Jean, "everyone else has cattle."

"We cannot afford cattle."

"We could have a calf, maybe."

"Even a calf is too much for us."

"A real calf perhaps. But we could have a calf of wood."

Ti-Jean set to. The calf he made stood on its four legs with its head down, as if it were grazing.

"It must go out to pasture with the rest of the cattle," Ti-Jean said.

The next day, when the cowherd came by, Ti-Jean called out to him, "I, too, own a calf now. I want you to take it to the fields."

The cowherd had no choice but to agree, for it was his job to tend the cattle of the villagers no matter what their standing.

"You will have to carry it," Ti-Jean told him. "The calf is far too young to walk."

The cowherd picked up the wooden calf in his arms. In the fields he put it down where the grass grew lush and green. All day it stood as if it were eating and eating.

When the time came for the cowherd to take the cattle back to the village, he called to them to follow, but, of course, Ti-Jean's calf made no move.

"Too bad for you," the cowherd shouted. "You can get home by yourself."

Ti-Jean was very angry when he found out what had happened. "You should not have left my calf behind," he said. "You are the cowherd! You will have to come back to the fields and help me get him."

By the time they got there, the calf had disappeared, although where it went the story does not say.

Now Ti-Jean was even angrier. He took his complaint to the mayor. The mayor decreed that the cowherd had been neglectful in his duties. He ordered the cowherd to give Ti-Jean a calf of his own to make up for the one that had been lost.

Ti-Jean and his wife were delighted with this arrangement. The calf they had been given grew strong all through the summer. Then the winter came. Ti-Jean and his wife were so poor that they had nothing to feed the creature. Worse still, they had nothing to eat themselves. In the end, although they were sorry to do it, they had to kill the calf for its meat.

The next morning, knowing there was a tanner in the nearby town and thinking the tanner might buy the calf skin for leather, Ti-Jean set off. As he traveled, he came upon a crow. The poor bird was shivering and half dead from the cold. Picking it up, Ti-Jean wrapped it in the calf skin to warm it. He carried the bird on with him, saving its life.

The weather had been harsh before, but now from across the river a storm blew up. The snow was falling so thickly that Ti-Jean decided to seek shelter in a nearby mill. The miller's wife was alone in the mill house.

"I have not much food to offer you," she said.

She gave Ti-Jean some bread and cheese to eat. She showed him a place in the corner where there was straw to lie on. Settling himself on the straw, he closed his eyes as if he were asleep. When a knock came at the door, he listened and peeked. To his surprise, he saw that the caller was the village priest.

"I have the wine all ready for us," the miller's wife said. "I have a roast of meat and potatoes and vegetables. I have baked a pie and cakes."

Ti-Jean thought then that he had been treated most shabbily, but he said nothing. Instead, he stayed quietly where he was. The priest was so eager, he took no notice of the sleeping man in the corner.

The miller's wife spread a fine white cloth on the table. She got out the best silver.

Just as she and the priest were about to sit down to feast together, the sound of someone putting a horse into the stable came from outside.

"It is my husband, home early," the miller's wife cried, jumping up.

Before Ti-Jean had time to catch his breath, she put the roast of meat behind the stove, the wine under one of the cushions, the potatoes and vegetables in a drawer in the dresser, and the pie and the cakes under the bed. She cleared away the cloth and the silver. She took the priest out to the summer kitchen and put him in the closet.

"I am so relieved to see you," Ti-Jean heard her say to her husband. "I was afraid the storm might harm you. Would that I had something good for you to eat."

Ti-Jean saw then that she was giving her husband just what he himself had been given—bread and cheese. The miller did not complain, but he did want to know who it was that was lying in the corner. The miller's wife said it was someone who had come in from the storm.

"Wake him and ask him if he would join me in my meal," the miller said.

Ti-Jean stretched and yawned and said he would be pleased to do so. As they were eating, the miller noticed the calf skin with the crow in it.

"What is it you have there?" he demanded.

"It is a magic bird," Ti-Jean said.

"Magic?" said the miller.

"Oh, yes," said Ti-Jean.

"How is it magic?"

Ti-Jean unwrapped the crow. By now the bird was feeling better. Its feathers were fluffed out, black and gleaming.

"It can foretell the future," Ti-Jean said.

"Foretell the future?"

"Five things it will know. Four it will say. The last it will hold secret."

"Show me," said the miller.

Ti-Jean pinched the crow behind its head. The crow let out a *krrk* of surprise.

"What does it speak of?" the miller asked.

"It says you do not have to eat bread and cheese, for there is a roast of meat behind the stove," Ti-Jean answered.

"A roast would be wonderful," said the miller. And, of course, the roast was found. "Ask about the second thing," the miller commanded.

Again Ti-Jean pinched the crow through its feathers. Again the bird let out its *krrk*.

"Well?" said the miller.

"There is a bottle of wine under one of the cushions," announced Ti-Jean.

"I should like to have wine," said the miller. "And the third thing?"

"There are potatoes and vegetables in the drawer of the dresser."

The table was becoming laden.

"A meal indeed," said the miller. "And the fourth?"

Ti-Jean gave the crow one more pinch. "Under the bed you will find pie and cakes," he said.

At this the miller's wife announced that she was too tired to sit with them any longer. She went off in fear and trembling.

"Can you not get the bird to tell us the fifth thing?" the miller demanded.

"It has found this fine meal for us. It would think we were ungrateful if we did not dine," Ti-Jean decreed.

"There must be something we can do to make the bird talk," the miller insisted, as soon as the meal was over.

"Well..." said Ti-Jean.

With that, he began to bargain. First the miller offered him one hundred, then two hundred and finally three hundred gold coins.

"That will do," he declared and pinched the crow again.

"What is it saying?" the miller demanded.

"It tells us the Devil is nearby," answered Ti-Jean. "He is in the closet in your summer kitchen."

"The Devil? We cannot live with the Devil."

Ti-Jean pretended to consider for a moment. "I think I can rescue you," he said.

Telling the miller to stay where he was, Ti-Jean went into the summer kitchen and opened the closet door.

"Be gone!" he cried. "Be gone!"

The priest ran off as quickly as he could.

"It was the Devil! It was!" said the miller. "I saw his long black robe."

In the morning, Ti-Jean set out with the three hundred gold coins in his pocket and the miller's cries of thanks in his ears. Ti-Jean and his wife were careful with the money. They wanted to make it last. Still, by spring, the villagers had begun to notice that certain improvements were being made to Ti-Jean's house. They saw that he and his wife no longer dressed in clothes that were full of patches and darns.

"He must have been to the place where golden snow falls," his neighbors told each other.

This was not good enough for the mayor. He called Ti-Jean to come and account for himself.

"I got my good fortune by going to sell my calf's skin," Ti-Jean explained.

"How much good fortune?" the mayor demanded.

"Three hundred gold pieces," Ti-Jean said.

Three hundred gold pieces! Word spread through the village. Everyone headed off to the nearby town in a great procession, the mayor among them. There was no need for the cowherd any longer. There were no more cattle; there were only cattle skins for sale.

The tanner offered not gold coins but pennies.

Ti-Jean was made to stand before the mayor again. He was accused of bringing ruin to his fellows. The villagers demanded he should be punished. He should be put into a barrel with holes in it and thrown into the nearest lake.

On the day of the punishment, Ti-Jean did not cry out or argue. He asked only that the priest be brought and a mass said for his soul. This priest was, of course, the same one who had visited the miller's wife.

The villagers drew apart in respect. Ti-Jean and the priest were alone.

"I saved you from your troubles," Ti-Jean said. "I ask you to promise to keep quiet and save me from mine."

It chanced that a shepherd was going by, driving a fine flock of sheep to market. When Ti-Jean saw him, he started shouting loudly, "No! No! No, I will not."

True to the promise, the priest said nothing. The shepherd, of course, wanted to know what was going on.

"I have been asked to be mayor," Ti-Jean answered. "It is not an honor I want, for first I must let myself be put into this barrel and let the barrel be put into the lake."

The shepherd thought he would like to be mayor.

"I will get into the barrel in your place," he offered.

"You must let no one see you," Ti-Jean said. "And you must let me have your sheep."

Ti-Jean hid. The shepherd got into the barrel. With the priest looking on, the villagers came and rolled the barrel into the water.

Imagine their surprise when they saw Ti-Jean driving the sheep through the village.

"Have you come up out of the lake?" they asked him.

"I have," he answered.

"How did you come by the sheep, then?"

"There is a land on the bottom of the lake—another world. When I climbed out of the barrel to walk around, I saw sheep everywhere. They filled the pretty meadows. There were so many, I did not think it would harm anyone if I took some for myself."

All the villagers wanted sheep, too. The mayor insisted, however, that he should be allowed to go into the lake first. It was a fine clear day—the sky all bright and blue and filled with small white clouds. The villagers saw the clouds reflected in the water.

"We see the sheep already," they cried.

Without waiting for the mayor to return, they followed after and—sad to say—each one of them drowned.

Ti-Jean and his wife lived happily from that day forward. They did not have to pretend to have what others had any longer. In fact, they were quite rich.

"We should remember not to get too greedy," Ti-Jean said to his wife, as he looked at their abundance.

And they did remember. They did not let themselves seek more, not ever, in all their lives.

SAYED'S BOOTS

EVERYONE brings something to a new country. Part of what Sayed brought was a terrible fear of never having enough. He had his reasons. In the small village he had come from, he had had so little.

He did not have little now. He lived in a big city. Through his intelligence and hard work, he had prospered. Still, the memories of his boyhood and his struggles would not leave him. He scrimped and saved far beyond what was needed. He was afraid to give away too much and so he gave away nothing. He kept all he possessed long after it should have been thrown out.

People who knew him saw this in the clothes he wore and the furniture he lived with. Mostly they saw it in the boots he faithfully pulled from his closet as each new winter approached. Those boots were the first good, truly warm pair he had bought himself.

But, oh, how battered they were; how patched and worn! There was hardly a scrap of the original material left in them. "Next winter," Sayed would say when someone suggested he might buy a new pair. The next winter went by and the next, but it was always the same. He would think about replacing the boots and then he would say to himself, "I only have to fix that eyelet. I only have to mend that hole, there, in the sole."

A year came when his trading was more successful than ever; a day came when he made himself an especially good deal. He met a friend in a small cafe and told him all about it.

"Do yourself a favor," his friend suggested. "Treat yourself. Get rid of those old things on your feet."

The friend would have gone with Sayed to the shoe store at that very moment, but Sayed was not certain. He looked and looked at his boots, but he could not make up his mind.

Anyway, it was time for prayer.

He had to go to the mosque. As he entered, he removed his footwear according to the custom. Many people had come to worship. There were pairs of boots and shoes of all shapes and sizes by the door.

Sayed set his own down among all the others. He went to his devotions, but when he was ready to leave, search as he might, his boots were nowhere to be found.

In the place where he thought he had left them, there was a brand-new pair. These were the finest boots that he had ever seen. They were just his size, too.

A smile came to his face as he became more and more certain that God had chosen to reward him. He slipped the boots on gratefully. Stepping out into the winter darkness, he went home.

He was eating his evening meal when he heard a knock at his door. Hoping it might be his friend and excited at the prospect of telling him about his good fortune, Sayed hurried to answer.

On the doorstep stood another man from his community—a leader, someone he did not know very well. This man was very angry indeed.

He wore a fine overcoat and a fine hat. He had fine gloves on his hands, but his feet were not so well covered, for he was wearing Sayed's old boots.

Sayed gave the new boots back at once.

"I knew these ones were yours, of course," the man burst out. "Everyone knows these boots. They are a shame! A disgrace!"

That was not the end of it, for the man was so outraged that he told everyone he could. Soon enough, everyone was laughing.

Sayed was ashamed. He bought new boots for himself, but the teasing still went on. Now there was nothing he wanted more than to be rid of those old boots that had been so precious to him.

He went to the bridge that crossed the frozen river. Tying the boots together, he threw them as far as he could onto the ice.

"They can freeze for all the trouble they've caused me," he thought to himself. "They can wait and wait through all the months of coldness. They will be swept away with the ice chunks in the end."

Spring came and the river melted. One day Sayed saw that there was only water flowing and churning where the boots had been. He wanted to dance, he was so relieved.

The relief did not last long. A friend went fishing and found the boots on the end of his line. When Sayed came home from work, the boots were outside his door as if they had been waiting for him. Everyone started laughing at him again.

He decided he would take the boots out and bury them. He would dig a hole deep under the bushes in a local park.

He waited until night fell and set off. A man saw him and believed he was doing something suspicious and called the police. Sayed was arrested and fined for causing mischief. The laughter grew louder.

"All this for a pair of boots," people chuckled.

Off he went to a place in the country where there was a smaller river. He threw the boots into the water.

All seemed to be going well until he saw a headline in the newspaper: "Town's water supply damaged." Under the headline there was an article about a channel being obstructed. Above the article, there was a photo of the cause.

This time Sayed's fine was even bigger because he had truly done damage. Even worse, the boots were still in his possession.

He would burn them. That was the only solution. In order to burn them, he had to dry them out. He put them in the sun in his front yard. A dog came by. It saw the boots, picked them up and shook them, and went running off with them in its mouth.

The dog ran into the road, almost causing an accident. It took the boots home and dropped them at the feet of the baby of the household. The baby grabbed them up and sucked on them. A piece came off and stuck in the baby's throat. The baby almost died.

Again Sayed was blamed. By now he was worrying about the boots so much that his business had begun to suffer. He was losing money all the time.

He thought about cutting the boots into tiny pieces with knives, or scissors, or even an ax. He thought about shredding them into fragments, boiling them in a pot, cooking them up to nothing—eating them for supper, even. Anything to be certain they would finally be gone.

At last it occurred to him that perhaps someone poor might find the boots useful. He went to the Thrift Shop to donate the boots, but the clerks there simply shook their heads. He went downtown among the street people, but even the street people did not want his gift.

Finally he came upon a man who was sitting in a doorway. This man was barefoot. Sayed offered the boots to him. The man took them, looked at them and threw them angrily in Sayed's face.

Sayed went home once more. He decided he would have to leave. If he couldn't get rid of the boots, he would have to go away from them. He put the boots in the closet and started packing.

Again there came a knock at his door. It was the friend who had wanted to help him get new boots in the beginning.

"Please," Sayed begged. "The old boots are ruining my life. Please save me from them. Please...please take them away."

The friend let out a laugh. "Why don't you just put the old boots in the garbage?" he suggested.

"It is not enough," Sayed answered.

"Of course it is," his friend replied.

Slowly Sayed picked up the boots. Slowly he went to the kitchen. He put the boots into a garbage bag, tied the bag tightly and carried it outside.

What happened next? The garbage was taken away and the boots went with it. The days turned into weeks and the weeks into months and the boots did not return.

Sometimes they came to Sayed in his dreams, but even that happened less and less often. Gradually he restored his business and made it more successful than it had ever been. Gradually people stopped laughing at him. At last he did not even dream of the boots.

Best of all, he began to change. He could not break himself of his old habits all at once, of course. Still, although he went on keeping his possessions longer than was needed, he learned how to get rid of them, too.

He found he was happier. He became more generous. In winter, he bought boots for those who were needy. Whenever he was asked, he gave money. When money was not enough, he sought out other ways to help.

PRADEEP AND THE PRINCESS LABAM

A T the edge of a small eastern city, on the banks of a river, there lived a boy whose name was Pradeep. His parents had come there from India when they were children. They had come with *their* parents. Pradeep had known no other home.

Pradeep was happy. He lived in a large house surrounded by green and open spaces. His grandparents were close enough for him to visit. He had plenty of friends; he lacked nothing.

His parents had one great fear for him, however. They were afraid that when he grew up, he would leave them and go away.

Whenever he went out, they told him, "You may walk as far as you want on those three sides, where there are meadows and we will always be able to see you. But on the fourth side, where there is forest, that way you may not go."

When he was small, this was no problem, but as Pradeep grew older, he found his parents' words harder and harder to obey. Often, on hot days, he would go to the forest's edge and stand gazing at the cool, dark shade there.

Finally he decided the warning could not have been meant to last forever. He would walk among the trees and see for himself what the forest was like.

He went a little way and then a little farther. He breathed the scent of the pines around him; he felt the soft brown needles underneath his feet.

Just as he was going to turn back, he saw a flash of red. He followed that color and found a bird that he had never seen before. The bird flew from tree to tree with Pradeep following.

"Why do you always go from me?" he called to it. "Why do you not stop?"

The bird settled on a branch above his head and hopped lower. It came to where he could almost reach out and stroke its feathers.

"How is it that you are here?" he demanded.

"The winds of the world have carried me," the bird replied.

Amazed to find the bird could speak, Pradeep questioned it further. "But where have you come from?"

"From the country of a princess."

"Which princess?"

"She is called the Princess Labam."

"Could I go there? Could I see her?"

The bird would say nothing more. It flew high into the sky. Pradeep thought that perhaps it was like the birds with bright plumage that his grandparents said came to their garden in India, but he could not be sure.

Pradeep went home. He did not wish to tell his parents what had happened, for he knew he would have to admit that he had disobeyed them. Still, he wondered about the princess. He wondered, too, about the country where she lived. In fact, he could think of nothing else. He abandoned his friends. His studies went unattended. He took to staying inside his room all day.

His mother became worried. When she saw how thin and pale he had grown, she asked him what was wrong. At first he said there was nothing, but then he had to tell her.

"You must have fallen asleep under the trees. You must have been dreaming," she decided.

"I was not dreaming," he declared.

His mother made him tell his father. "Birds do not talk," his father argued. "That is all stuff of your grandparents' stories—their tales of long ago."

His father's arguments only made Pradeep more eager.

"There must be some place where birds still talk," he answered. "After all, I heard this bird with my own ears."

His longing grew deeper. Finally he came to his parents and told them, "If I do not try to find the princess and her country, I shall die."

His parents were troubled. "You do not even know which way to go," they insisted.

"I shall enter the forest. I shall walk until the way becomes clear to me," Pradeep proclaimed.

"Promise us just one thing," his parents begged. "Promise you will return to us."

"I promise willingly that if I am not killed on the way, I will come back to you," Pradeep agreed.

What could his parents do? They helped him gather together the things he needed. They bought him clothes for traveling and gave him money for the journey. His mother went to the kitchen. Although she shed many tears as she was working, she cooked food for him. Taking nuts and milk and spices and sugar, she made golden *perhas* and pistachio *barfi*—the special treats she knew he loved.

At last the day came for Pradeep to leave. He did then as he had said he would. He simply began to walk. He went first into the forest. He looked for the bird, but it was gone. The forest did not stretch far. Soon he had hard road beneath his feet. The road took him beside the river. Still he kept walking.

On and on he went. When the sun was high in the sky, he stopped to eat. To finish his meal, he opened up the sweetmeats his mother had given him. Just as he was about to take out one of the small diamond-shaped pieces of *barfi*, an ant ran onto it.

"The ant must be hungry," Pradeep thought.

Leaving that first piece of *barfi* untouched, he reached for another. As he did so, a second ant appeared. So it went on, over and over, until he had given away all of the *barfi* and all of the *perhas* as well.

As he was about to get up, an ant that was larger than the others came and stood before him. To his surprise the ant could speak.

"You have been kind and generous," it said to him. "If you should need help, you have only to think of us and we will come to your aid."

Pradeep thanked the ant, even though he could not imagine how he would ever need help from creatures so small.

He walked that day and into the next one. He followed more roads. He skirted fields and crossed bridges over streams. He plodded up hills and down into valleys.

As he went, the way grew wilder. He came to another forest where the trees were older and the light beneath them dimmer. The darkness made him shiver but he did not give up.

As he journeyed through this forest, he heard the crying of an animal. It seemed like a large animal, but still he went toward the sound. He found a great rock with a niche in it. A bear was sitting outside the niche. It was the bear that had been crying, for it was in much pain.

By now, Pradeep was used to talking animals.

"What is the matter?" he asked.

"A sliver of wood has gone into my paw," the bear answered. "I cannot get it out."

"I could try to help you, but you would have to promise not to harm me," Pradeep said.

The bear gave the promise readily enough. When Pradeep looked, he saw that one of the bear's paws was sore and swollen—so swollen the sliver could not be seen.

"I shall have to cut your foot with this," Pradeep said, showing the bear his pocket knife.

As he cut, of course, he made the bear's pain greater. The bear cried even more loudly.

Just as Pradeep managed to pull out the sliver, he heard another animal coming. This one seemed even larger.

"It is my mother," the bear explained. "She will have heard me and she will be angry. You must go into our den until I tell her what you have done."

Pradeep hid in the niche in the rock. He watched the mother bear coming. She had a second young bear with her. They were moving quickly, fiercely.

True to its word, the first bear told her how it had been helped. The mother bear called for Pradeep to come out so she could thank him. He stayed for three days until he could be certain the wound in the first bear's paw would heal.

"I must leave now," he announced then.

"You have saved my son's life," the mother bear said to him. "If he could not walk to find food, he would surely die. Think of us, if ever you should need us. Think of us and we will come." Pradeep said he would do this.

In the forest he came to a clearing. In the clearing there was an old house. As Pradeep drew nearer to the house, he heard quarreling. Outside in the yard, he saw four young men.

"Why are you quarreling?" he asked.

The young men stopped their quarrel to speak to him.

"Our father has died," the oldest told him. "He has left us four objects of magic. The first is a bed that will carry whoever sits upon it wherever he wants to go. The second is a bag that will give to its owner whatever he asks for. The third is a bowl that will always fill with water. The fourth is a stick with a rope wrapped around it. If you say the words, 'Stick, beat those who are coming against me,' the stick will do that. If you say, 'Rope, tie them up'—even if it is a large army—that, too, will be done."

"So why are you quarreling?" Pradeep said.

"Our father did not say which of us should have the bed and which the bag, which the bowl and which the stick and the rope," the youngest explained.

Pradeep thought of how tired his feet were. He thought of how he did not know where he was going. He thought of how he had to see the Princess Labam and her country. He vowed to himself that, if he lived, he would repay the young men somehow.

"I could help you," he offered.

"How could you help us?"

Pradeep said. "My father is a lawyer. I could give you a judgment—a ruling."

The quarreling sons looked pleased.

"A judgment is a serious matter. I cannot do it if I am hungry," Pradeep went on.

"We can make food for you," the sons offered.

"That would be good," said Pradeep. "I will wait outside. I will look at the magic objects and consider. As soon as I have eaten, the judgment will be made."

The four young men went into the house. Hardly had the door closed behind them when Pradeep picked up the magic bag. Hesitating for only a moment, he picked up the bowl and the stick and the rope also. Then he sat on the magic bed.

"Carry me to the Princess Labam's country," he commanded.

At once, Pradeep was borne over prairies and seas and mountains. When the bed landed at last, he knew that he was in another country indeed. All about him were scents that reminded him of his mother's garden when the mock orange bushes and the roses were blooming, but these scents were so much stronger. Everywhere he looked he saw that there were flowers in a myriad of rich hues.

Pradeep hid the bed behind a small bush. Taking the bag and the bowl, the stick and the rope with him, he walked until he came to a village. He knocked on the door of the first house.

An old woman answered. She was dressed in a sari. It was plainer than the ones his grandmother wore for special occasions, but it was exactly the same style.

"I am lost," he said to her. "Please, I ask you to tell me where I am."

Her answer was the one he had been hoping for. "You are in the country of the Princess Labam." Still, she looked frightened. "You cannot stay," she said.

"Why not?" he asked her.

"Strangers are not allowed in the country of the Princess Labam."

"But I am so tired."

"The king does not permit it."

Pradeep begged and pleaded. "Could you not let me stay for just one night?" he asked.

"You must promise that you will go in the morning," the old woman told him.

"I promise! I promise!" Pradeep cried out.

With that the old woman welcomed him in. Her house was spotless, everything in order. She went to prepare him a meal.

"Sit, Grandmother," he insisted. "I will do all that is required."

He did, too. He put his hand inside the magic bag.

"Bag," he commanded. "Give us a fine dinner."

Food appeared in abundance. Dish after dish came—each made of the very best ingredients, each spiced to perfection, each served on a platter of gold. The old woman dined with relish, for this was a meal beyond her dreams.

"I will go to get water for us to drink," she said when they had finished eating.

"I will give you water," Pradeep replied. He commanded the magic bowl to fill itself, and the water that flowed into it was pure and sweet.

Night was coming by then. With the night the scents of the flowers outside grew even stronger, filling the air.

"Should I light a lamp for you?" Pradeep asked.

"Oh, no!" the old woman answered. "The king forbids it, and anyway there is no need. We will have light soon enough. You will see."

"How can you have light without lamps?"

"The light is given by the Princess Labam herself," said the old woman. "At nightfall she goes to the rooftop of the palace. She sits there and she shines like the moon for us. She makes the dark as bright as day. She stays on the rooftop until midnight, so we can finish the work we have to do. She goes to her room then and all of the kingdom sleeps."

Pradeep's excitement knew no bounds. "Will I see her?" he demanded.

"You may look through the window," the old woman told him. "But you must not be seen yourself so you cannot go outside."

Pradeep kept watch. He saw the princess come to the rooftop. He saw the light that shone from her.

"How beautiful she is," he murmured to himself.

When the Princess Labam went in, he waited. As soon as he was certain the old woman was fast asleep, he crept out. He came to the bush. There was the magic bed just as he had left it.

"Take me to the Princess Labam herself," he said.

Before he knew it, he was in the room where the princess was sleeping. This room was far more luxurious than anything Pradeep had ever seen. There were curtains of silk with gold embroidery; there were carpets of wondrous colors; there was a lattice of gleaming marble inlaid with jewels.

Pradeep's eyes were fixed on the princess, for she looked even more beautiful to him now that he was close by. He watched and watched, not wanting to disturb her. He knew she was the one he loved. Overcome with the wish to have something to give her, he put his hand into the magic bag. He thought of the flowers outside; he thought again of the flowers in his mother's garden.

"I must have the brightest and most fragrant roses for her," he decreed.

The bag filled and refilled itself. Taking the roses in his hands, Pradeep strewed them everywhere; he placed them all around the room.

Light was coming into the sky, and so he knew that he must leave. Riding on the magic bed, he made his way back to the old woman's house. Just in time, for she was almost waking. When she did, she spoke to him.

"Truly," she said, "truly, now you must go."

Pradeep made his voice sound weaker. "Oh, Grandmother," he answered. "I am so sorry, but today I am sick." He made himself look sick, too. Again the old woman took pity on him. "You will not regret it," he assured her. "I shall have the bag bring us more good things to eat. I shall have the bowl bring us water as well."

Meanwhile, of course, the princess had woken. She had seen the roses filling her room. She had called her servants; she had asked the king and the queen how such a thing might have happened, but no one could say.

All through the day, Pradeep waited. He longed to go out and explore this country he had come to, but he did not. At nightfall, he stood by the window again. When he saw the Princess Labam on the rooftop of the palace, his heart was filled with joy. In awe and reverence, he gazed at her for as long as she stayed there. He grieved when she went in and took her light away.

Just as before, he remained in the house until he was sure the old woman was sleeping. Then he ran to the magic bed.

"Take me! Oh, take me to the princess," he cried out.

The bed obeyed at once. Pradeep wanted so much to touch the princess and speak to her, but he did not do so. He simply stayed with her all through the night and, before he left, he put his hand into the magic bag. There were so many gifts he could have given her but she seemed to have so much. At last he decided it must be a gift from his own country. It must be a picture of the sun shining on the snow in winter.

Gently he placed the picture on the pillow beside her. Reluctantly, at the first gray light of morning, he told the bed to carry him away.

By this time the old woman was more anxious than ever to have him leave.

"We are both in danger," she told him.

"One more day, Grandmother," he pleaded. "One more, for still I am not fully well."

The old woman was swayed both by her pity and by the fine food Pradeep had given her.

"Tomorrow," she insisted.

"Oh, yes! Tomorrow!" he said.

Again through the hours of daylight he waited, but the princess was always in his mind. He imagined her awakening to the picture and delighting in it. He imagined her puzzlement about where it had come from. In this he was not mistaken, for she had questioned all who could be questioned, and still had found no clue.

The third night came. Once more he watched as she sat on the palace rooftop. Once more he used the magic bed to go to her room.

"I would have a beautiful ring for her," he told the magic bag.

On this night he could not resist. Instead of leaving the ring on her pillow, he tried to put it on her finger. He was as careful as he could be, but still he woke her. When she first saw him, she put her hands to her face in terror. She was so frightened that she was about to summon her guards.

"Please," he said. "Please wait, for it is I who brought the flowers and the picture to you."

He told her then of the bird that had spoken to him—"a bird of your country." He told her of his long journey and how he had refused to give up. As the princess listened, she heard the love in his voice. Even before the dawn, they knew they wished to stay together as long as they might live.

"I will tell my father," the princess said. "I will say I have found the one I want to marry. First, though, you must leave. You must wait until a messenger comes for you. My father must not find you here."

Pradeep went back to the old woman's house. When she woke, he told her the great news. To his surprise, she looked more frightened than ever.

"Are you not pleased for me?" Pradeep demanded.

"You do not understand," the old woman answered. "Wherever you have come from, you should go back there. You should go back as quickly as you can."

"But, why?" Pradeep asked. "Why, when I am so happy?"

"When a suitor comes, the king sets tasks for him such as no one can accomplish. It is true that if you succeed he will let you marry his daughter, but it is also true that if you fail he will have you killed."

"Why did the princess not speak to me of this?"

"Perhaps she was afraid you would leave her," the old woman answered.

Pradeep thought of his home with its green and open spaces. He thought of the safety he had known there. He thought of the Princess Labam's beauty and his love for her.

"I cannot give up now," he decided. "I cannot let her down."

Finally, one of the royal servants came to summon him to the king's court.

"If you wish to marry the princess," said the king, "I must know that you are worthy. You must be able to do great deeds. Out in the courtyard, my servants have prepared for you a mound of mustard seeds. You must crush them into oil by this same hour tomorrow. If you do not, you will lose your life."

When Pradeep saw the seeds his heart sank, for they were piled up almost as high as he was tall. And what did he know about crushing mustard seeds? What had his life in his own country taught him about that?

Hoping she might be able to help him, he went to the old woman.

"No one can do so much in just one day," she told him, shaking her head.

Despair fell on him. It came to him that he would never see his parents again. He thought of how anxious they had looked when he had left them. He thought of the sweetmeats his mother had cooked for him.

With the thought of the sweetmeats he remembered the ants in the forest so far away.

At once, the chief ant appeared before him.

"Why are you so sad? What is the matter?" the ant asked.

"I must crush these seeds, and I must do it before tomorrow morning. If I cannot, I shall be killed."

"For ants, such a task is easy. Rest, sleep. The work will be accomplished soon enough."

More ants came. They came in the hundreds and thousands. The seeds were crushed in no time.

In the morning, when Pradeep went to the king, he presented him with the mustard seed oil in a large jar.

"That is only the first test," the king told him. "Now you must kill the demons I keep locked in a cage in my cellar. I shall have my servants take you down there. By tomorrow it must be done."

Pradeep was led down into the cellar. The demons were horrible monsters.

"Who am I against them?" Pradeep burst out.

Certain that the demons would surely kill him if he tried to fight them, he put his head in his hands in sorrow. Even as he sat grieving, he remembered the bears. He pictured their home in the rock. He pictured the mother bear's great strength.

Just as they had promised, the bears were with him in an instant.

"How can we help you?" they asked.

"I must kill these demons," Pradeep answered. "If I cannot, I shall be killed myself."

"Have the servants open the cage," the mother bear commanded.

Pradeep did so. The mother bear and the two young bears entered the cage and fought and fought. It did not happen quickly, but at last the demons were dead.

"The tasks are not over," the king insisted when Pradeep told him of his success. "In the sky I have a magic kettledrum. You must go up there and beat on it. If you fail, I will see to it that you die."

For Pradeep, this task was not so difficult, because he had the magic bed. He went to where it was and climbed on.

"Take me to the king's kettledrum," he commanded.

The bed obeyed. Pradeep beat on the drum as loudly as he was able, and then he came down.

The king was not pleased. He took Pradeep to where an old tree had fallen in the palace gardens. The tree had a trunk so thick that three men with outstretched arms could not have surrounded it. Into Pradeep's hands the king put a small ax made of wax.

"The trunk of the tree must be split in half," he ordered. "It must be done by this same hour tomorrow. If it is not, I shall have my servants take your life."

The bears could not help Pradeep; the ants could not help him. The magic bag and the bowl, the stick and the rope, and the bed were of no use.

That day he said goodbye to the old woman. That night he commanded the magic bed to take him to the Princess Labam's room one last time.

"Tomorrow I go to my death," he told her with tears in his eyes.

"How can this be?" she asked.

"Your father has set me a task I cannot accomplish. Try as I might, in this I cannot succeed."

"Tell me of the task," the princess said.

Pradeep told her. He showed her the small ax. He described for her the thickness of the tree.

"Do not give up hope," said the princess, and she pulled a long, dark hair from the top of her head. "When you go to the tree, go by yourself," she ordered. "Lay this hair from my head along the edge of the ax's blade. Make sure no one can hear you. Say to the tree, 'The Princess Labam commands you to allow yourself to be cut.'"

Pradeep did as he was told. He went to the tree by himself. He stretched the hair along the blade of the waxen ax. He called out to the tree, "The Princess Labam commands you to allow yourself to be cut." He watched in amazement, for as soon as the hair touched the tree, the trunk split in two.

Now the king had to agree that Pradeep could marry the princess, and soon the wedding took place. There was much feasting and rejoicing. Pradeep made sure the old woman was invited. He gave her a place of honor. He told the Princess Labam about his country. He explained about the picture. He saw her eyes light up.

"I must go to see my parents, for I promised," he told her.

"I must come with you," she insisted.

"The ways will seem strange to you."

"I will learn whatever I have to," she declared.

She went then to tell her father she was leaving. Since he truly wished his daughter well, he gave her and Pradeep much wealth. Of course, to make the journey, they climbed onto the magic bed.

Pradeep's parents were pleased indeed to see them. They welcomed the princess with delight. Pradeep's grandparents came. His friends came and his neighbors. There was more rejoicing and more feasting.

"I believe we should live here, in your country," the Princess Labam said when all was done.

Pradeep told her he must return the magic objects. She wanted to go on that journey, too. Pradeep gave the four young men some of his new riches to thank them. He told them his judgment was that they should share the objects among them. He laughed when he thought of how he had not used the stick and rope at all.

The young men took Pradeep and the princess home. It was their last ride on the magic bed. After that they lived happily. Sometimes they went walking in the forest. Often they spoke together of how everything had started with the bright red bird.

Pradeep worked hard again at his studies. Much changed, but the love between him and the Princess Labam did not. She no longer shone from the rooftop, but she still gave light to him. In fact, in that small city she shone for all who knew her. She gave forth light by day as well as by night.

A NOTE ON SOURCES

THE FOREST BRIDE

A story originating in Finland and found in *Best-Loved Folk-Tales of the World*, selected and with an introduction by Joanna Cole (New York: Anchor Books/Doubleday, 1982, pp. 387-394). Cole's source is Parker Filmore's *The Shepherd's Nosegay*, edited by Katherine Love (New York: Harcourt Brace Jovanovich, 1950).

MARIA'S GIFT

From *Best-Loved Folk-Tales of the World*, selected and with an introduction by Joanna Cole (New York: Anchor Books/Doubleday, 1982, pp. 186-190). Cole's story is entitled "The Twelve Months" and comes from Georgios A. Megas's *Folktales of Greece* in The Folktales of the World Series, edited by Richard M. Dorson (University of Chicago Press, 1970).

THE FLY

From *Best-Loved Folk-Tales of the World*, selected and with an introduction by Joanna Cole (New York: Anchor Books/Doubleday, 1982, pp. 572-575). Cole has taken the story from Mai Vo-Dinh, *The Toad Is the Emperor's Uncle, Animal Folktales from Viet-Nam* (Sung Ngo-Dinh, 1970). Thanks are due to author Judy Fong Bates who reviewed the story in terms of her experience as a child growing up in Ngoc's situation; also to Thao Duong of the Vietnamese Canadian Federation who read the story for authenticity and offered encouragement.

THE PINCOYA'S CHILD

Storyteller and children's writer Celia Lottridge told this story at a weekend retreat. She said she knew I would love it and she was right. She found the story in a school textbook in a series entitled The Dolch Folklore of the World, written by Edward W. Dolch and Marguerite P. Dolch (Champagne, Illinois: Garrard Publishing Co.). She believes the book was called *Stories from Chile* but neither of us has so far been able to find it again. Thanks to Chilean Canadian Maria Eugenia Otarola who read my version for authenticity.

THE COUPLE'S JOURNEY

I heard this story from Omushkego elder Penishish—Louis Bird. He has spent many years collecting the stories of his people. He taped this one for me and made sure it found its right form. He says the story has many different versions and ways of telling. In its original it would have been much longer, with complete episodes recounting the couple's various adventures. It might thus have filled the long evenings when the Omushkego were in the small family hunting camps between the end of September and the beginning of June. Or it might have been told over the seasons— summer being the time for the events up to the couple's marriage, winter for a portion of their journey, for example.

WISE FATHER, WISE DAUGHTER

A story I learned first from storyteller Itah Sadu. When she was telling the story, she said it had its origins in Zimbabwe, a country to which she went traveling in her storytelling work.

LITTLE DAUGHTER OF THE SNOW

One of Arthur Ransome's *Old Peter's Russian Tales* (London: Puffin Books, 1974, pp. 93-103). The song is unchanged because I could not imagine any storyteller telling any version of the story without it.

TI-JEAN AND THE CALF

A tale from the Brothers Grimm to be found in *The Complete Grimm's Fairy Tales*, with an introduction by Padraic Colum (New York: Pantheon Books/Random House, 1972, pp. 311-316). The Grimm's story is called "The Little Peasant."

SAYED'S BOOTS

Taken from a story entitled "Abu Kasem's Slippers," recorded and discussed in Heinrich Zimmer's *The King and the Corpse: Tales of the Soul's Conquest of Evil*, edited by Joseph Campbell (Bollingen Series XI. Princeton: Princeton University Press, 1993, pp. 9-25). The story there is set in Baghdad and has in turn been taken from *Thamarat ul-Awrak* (Fruits of Leaves) by Ibn Hijjat al-Hamawi. A second rendering into English is noted as being found in *Other Arabian Nights* by H.I. Katibah (New York: Charles Scribner's Sons, 1928). Gratitude is expressed to author and storyteller Rukhsana Khan for her advice about the Muslim aspects of the tale.

Pradeep and the Princess Labam

One more from *Best-Loved Folk-Tales of the World*, selected and with an introduction by Joanna Cole (New York: Anchor Books/Doubleday, 1982, pp. 583-591). The original story is called "How the Raja's Son Won the Princess Labam." Thanks go to author Rachna Gilmore for her assistance in detailing the sights and scents of the Princess Labam's country.